CW01457225

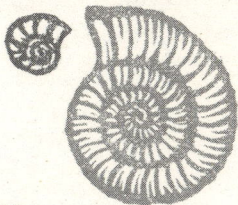

Out There in the WILD

POEMS ON NATURE

Out There in the WILD

POEMS ON NATURE

Nicola Davies, James Carter and Dom Conlon

Illustrated by Diana Catchpole

MACMILLAN CHILDREN'S BOOKS

Published 2023 by Macmillan Children's Books
an imprint of Pan Macmillan
The Smithson, 6 Briset Street, London EC1M 5NR
EU representative: Macmillan Publishers Ireland Ltd, 1st Floor,
The Liffey Trust Centre, 117–126 Sheriff Street Upper
Dublin 1, D01 YC43
Associated companies throughout the world
www.panmacmillan.com

ISBN 978-1-0350-0406-5

Text copyright © Nicola Davies, James Carter and Dom Conlon 2023
Illustrations copyright © Diana Catchpole 2023

The right of Nicola Davies, James Carter, Dom Conlon and Diana Catchpole to be
identified as the authors and illustrator of this work has been asserted by them
in accordance with the Copyright, Designs and Patents Act 1988.

All rights reserved. No part of this publication may be reproduced,
stored in a retrieval system, or transmitted, in any form or by any means
(electronic, mechanical, photocopying, recording or otherwise),
without the prior written permission of the publisher.

Pan Macmillan does not have any control over, or any responsibility for,
any author or third-party websites referred to in or on this book.

1 3 5 7 9 8 6 4 2

A CIP catalogue record for this book is available from the British Library.

Printed and bound by CPI Group (UK) Ltd, Croydon CR0 4YY

MIX
Paper | Supporting
responsible forestry
FSC® C116313
FSC
www.fsc.org

This book is sold subject to the condition that it shall not, by way of trade or otherwise,
be lent, resold, hired out, or otherwise circulated without the publisher's prior consent in
any form of binding or cover other than that in which it is published and without a similar
condition including this condition being imposed on the subsequent purchaser.

Pour les Petits Fours — MM, Notty Chris & the Ivy Bee.
Massive thanks as ever to Professor Graham Denton.
—J. C.

For Julia and David, Val and Nell, Vicki,
Chris and Rosa in celebration of life and love.
—N. D.

For Oliver, through season, storm and shelter.
—D. C.

Contents

Introduction   xii

The Rhythm   *James*   2

Out There in the Wild

You're out there	*James*	7
Pacific Navigators	*Nicola*	8
The Colour of the Hills	*Nicola*	9
The Light	*James*	10
You and the World	*Dom*	11
Watching the Weather	*Nicola*	13
A bowlful of fire	*Dom*	14
New Town	*Dom*	15
Inuit Parka in the British Museum	*Nicola*	16
New Gold	*Dom*	17
Oil	*Dom*	20
The time my dog and I were stopped by a stranger	*Dom*	22
Dog Years	*Dom*	23
The receipt from the zoo gift shop	*Dom*	24
We are not who we were	*Dom*	26
Balance	*Dom*	27
Underneath the City the Whale Swims	*Nicola*	28
Even in the rain	*James*	29
Looking now at the poinsettia	*Dom*	31
Thanks to gravity	*James*	32
Haiku from a Train	*James*	33

The hug	*Dom*	34
How to choose a pet	*Dom*	35
Grandpa's Dogs	*Nicola*	36
How to move like a rock	*Dom*	37

Where Sunlight Sifts Cliff and Sky

The Book of British Birds	*Nicola*	41
Every night	*James*	42
Why Humans?	*Nicola*	43
Finch	*Dom*	44
Peregrine	*Nicola*	45
Swift by your Side	*Dom*	46
Crow	*James*	48
Isn't it incredible	*James*	49
Motorway Cinquain	*James*	51
Listen to the one who doesn't write poetry	*Dom*	52
Manx Shearwater	*Nicola*	53
Gannets	*Nicola*	54
Choughs at Marloes	*Nicola*	55
Swan	*Dom*	56
Feral Canada Geese	*Nicola*	57
Without a name	*James*	58
The Nest	*James*	60
Bird and boy	*Dom*	62

The Deep, Deep Blue

Ammonite	*Nicola*	67
Just One Place	*Nicola*	68
Paddling	*Dom*	69

The Pond	*James*	70
River	*James*	72
The Bucket	*James*	73
Limpet	*Nicola*	74
Lantern Fishes	*Nicola*	75
Night-Time Reef	*Nicola*	77
The Emperor's Ice	*Nicola*	78
Narwhal Sonnet	*Nicola*	79
Greenland Shark	*Dom*	80
52 Blue – The Loneliest Whale	*Dom*	82
Cerulean	*Dom*	84
Which creature would you be?	*James*	85

Green Song

Green Song	*Nicola*	89
It's Not Hard to Make a Forest	*Nicola*	90
Seasons 4	*James*	91
The Tree Whale	*Dom*	92
Tree	*James*	94
The Old Wood	*James*	95
Grass Dance	*Dom*	96
Hay Making	*Nicola*	97
'. . . take only pictures, leave only footprints . . .'	*James*	98

Plant an Acorn Now to Give Your Grandchildren Shade

There will always still be sky	*Nicola*	101
What Will You Remember When You Are Old?	*Nicola*	102

Animal Alphabet	*Nicola*	104
Who cares	*James*	105
A Song for the Future, a Song for the Past	*Dom*	106
When	*Nicola*	107
Rude Boys Rinsed	*Nicola*	108
Can There Be Sky?	*Nicola*	109
Tomorrow, Today	*Nicola*	110

Across the Land with a Leap and a Bound

Still	*Nicola*	115
Mountain Hare	*Dom*	116
Somewhere	*James*	117
The Sun and the Hare	*Dom*	118
Fox, what have you done?	*James*	119
Batswoopswoop	*Dom*	120
I'm Beastly, Me	*James*	122
If you've ever seen a wolf	*James*	124
She watches the world	*James*	126
Come On Out	*James*	128
My First Badger	*Nicola*	130

Home is Wherever Your Spirit is Free

Gorilla Gazing	*James*	133
Yes, it was the Romans	*James*	135
The Monkey and the Apple	*James*	136
Elephant	*James*	138
Elephant Smile	*Dom*	140
Giraffe	*Dom*	141
Home	*James*	142

How Many Minibeasts?

How Many Minibeasts?	*James*	147
Sugar the bee and me	*Dom*	148
September Haiku	*James*	149
The Holy Rollers	*James*	150
Glow Worms	*Nicola*	152
Woodlice	*Nicola*	153
Dragon Fly	*Nicola*	154
Spider, Spider . . .	*James*	155
Stick Insect	*Dom*	156

Wonder

Whether you call it magic	*James*	161
Quetzalcoatlus	*Nicola*	162
Have you ever	*James*	163
Up Uffington Hill	*James*	164
Selkie Summoning	*Nicola*	166
Talking Hands	*James*	168
We'll never know	*James*	169

Index of First Lines	173
About the Poets	178
About the Illustrator	179
Acknowledgements	180

Introduction

Sometimes I will sit in a field, hoping to catch sight of a hare or deer. Around me the long grass whispers warnings to the animals that might approach me and I'm left alone. Yet as the sound of crickets strikes the flint of my imagination I wonder: am I just looking at nature or am I part of nature?

It's easy to believe that humans are outside of nature. I don't have to use my springy leg muscles to race after a deer and capture it for food. I'm part of a species which has learned to farm, to manufacture. I don't have to leap out of a nest in order to fly. I can book a ticket on a plane and explore places which were undiscovered until recently. Or I can turn on the television and learn all about lions and tigers and bears. Humans are inventive. But as humans we risk our own future when we see ourselves as just looking at nature. We are part of nature. As much a part as the tree is for the woodlouse, or the soil is for the potato.

This book explores all connections we have with life on this planet. 'There's a rhythm out there / there's a rhythm within / as the seasons turn / as the planets spin' as James Carter writes. Nicola Davies, Diana Catchpole and myself join James to follow this rhythm in our own ways. It takes Nicola from 'gleams of plankton' to an old man and his dog, her ten-year-old self, and the absolute wonder of 'a whale that leaps and turns into a swan'.

James follows the rhythm through the sun and the moon, dragonflies, bees and bats, the swoop of an owl 'beneath a blue-black sea of night', and 'a weave of love' – a nest.

I find the rhythm like a path. It leads me to foxes at 3 a.m., the gold of honey and daffodils, mountain hares who 'leap from the lea / ahead of the fox's shadow', that 'ancient tree of the sea' the Greenland shark, and the curious friendship of a boy and a bird. And Diana, through her illustrations, reminds us of a time when humans lived in balance with the rest of nature. Her lines are rhythm itself, conjuring the flicker of fires in caves and the passage of swallows across the sky.

These poems are all written with thought and humour and love. We hope they become part of your life.

Dom

The Rhythm

There's a rhythm out there
there's a rhythm within
as the seasons turn
as the planets spin

It's the call of the wild
it's the breath of the world
and it's life so alive
that it has to be heard

It's the sweep of the swoop
of the owl at dawn
it's the dash of the fox
through the August corn

There's a rhythm out there . . .

It's the tug of the breeze
and the tree that it shakes
and the nest and the egg
and the crack as it breaks

It's the river that rolls
as it picks up pace
it's the moon and the sea
and those great grey waves

There's a rhythm out there . . .

It's the melody's chant
and the harmony's chime
as our pulses dance
to the tick of time

It's the feet of the child
as it steps in line
to the beat of the song
to the ring of the rhyme

There's a rhythm out there
and it comes from our drum
from our home – from our star
and it's called . . . T H E   S U N !

James

Out There in the Wild

You're out there, in the wild,
   a little lost maybe. Even ghost-breath
cold. Deep in an animal-now, knowing

only of that instant. Your senses
   feral-alert to detect a conker-fall
from a field away; catch a glimpse

of a red kite's shadow shooting over
   a hill; hold just the briefest gaze
with a deer; spot a kingfisher slicing

the afternoon in half. But time fades.
   And you'll be useless in the ever-fuzzy
country darkness. So you'll drift back

in the direction of home, now aware
   that you're all by yourself, and tired, yet
also more awake than when you left.

You're never as alive
   as when you're in the wild.

                                              James

Pacific Navigators

Once, on the blue side of the world
people learned a list of stars to guide them,
and tuned their skins
to the criss-cross conversations of the waves.
They divined the clues in fish shoals, flocks of birds,
gleams of plankton,
and understood what the clouds told them.
With a thousand threads of noticing,
they found themselves,
and land like scattered seed in all that blue.
That's the kind of knowing that we've lost,
Now satellites can find us anywhere
but we can't find ourselves.

Nicola

The Colour of the Hills

What colour are the hills?
Not blue, like a school jersey.
Not grey, like next door's cat.
Not purple, like a bruise.
You can't name their colour, only feel it.
Like a dream at midnight,
Or a half-remembered song –
If you try to put a word to it
It slips away.
So when people ask you
'What colour are the hills?'
Just shrug, say nothing;
Hold their colour,
Unnamed in your heart.

Nicola

The Light

We live
  for the light.

Like flowers,
  our heads
ever turn
  where it's bright.

We yearn when dark
  for the planet to spin,
for the light to return
  and for life to begin.

Without it,
  we wither.
We sleepwalk
  through winter.

Moon, tell the sun
  to spark out the night.
We need to be loved,
  be touched by the light.

James

You and the World

There's a path you must find
but the Earth will be kind
so know that you're never alone.

Just look to the ground
and you'll know that you've found
a place which you can call home.

There's a chasm to cross
but don't be put off —
there are bridges each step of the way.

Just look to the seed,
at how it is freed
to fly on a wild, windy day.

There's a mountain to climb
but slow, take your time —
nature gave you all that you need.

Just look to the tree
at how that can be
grown from a very small seed.

Let the world look to you
in whatever you do
as you look after the Earth.

Just be all you are
and you will go far
as you grow from the moment of birth.

Dom

Watching the Weather

He was a solitary child
Who ran everywhere,
Watched the tide creep in, silver through the muddy channels,
And thought about the territory of clouds.
Words were always tricky,
Other people, distant,
Blurred against the sharpness of the hills, the sky.
Figures spoke to his heart:
Windspeed, rainfall, humidity and temperature,
Eloquent expressions of the deep, majestic conversation
Held between the land, the air, the sea.
Time has layered him with weathers.
Given him a skin of wind and rain,
So complex and so subtle
That he can touch the air and know
How your feet will fall upon the mountain,
How the air will caress you in the glen.
And the greatest wonder?
Now words please him as much as numbers,
and people are as close and clear as hills.

Nicola

13

A bowlful of fire

who'd have thought a flame could find a home in water and
yet I have watched two of them swim like twin suns reflected
in an astronaut's helmet, weaving the blue space and twisting
the words of the fairground man who said they would forget
everything every three seconds forget everything every three
seconds forget that I saw them remember the shape of the
ripples on that lake six years ago when dad rowed us leaning to
and fro back and forth to tell us stories of our grandfather going
to war coming back from war going to work coming back from
work going on holiday coming back from holiday his light
swimming through our father's life like a lighthouse guiding
him to shore a mile or more from his fire-ringed island

Dom

New Town

3 a.m. and a hush of bin bags splits the night
like fishermen spilling their oily catch
onto the tarmac's dry sea.

The dog barks. The gulls wait. A light
guides sleepy eyes to the red dawn
of the fox's fur.

This town tries to hold back the tide,
to define the ebb and flow of life and yet
the rock pools here are rich.

Dom

Inuit Parka in the British Museum

I love this parka in its big glass case.
It is so well designed.
Its hood would never slip,
nor its shoulders pull.
Transparent, leaf-light,
waterproof and breathable,
better than some top-end Gore-tex jacket.
It's made from seal –
from the membrane, one cell thick that lines the gut,
seams sewn with sinew
to swell when wet and keep them watertight.
It embodies knowledge, intimate as love,
the ingenuity of need: that nothing can be wasted
and if you take too much, you'll perish.
It is a symbol of all we have forgotten,
and everything we need to learn.

Nicola

New Gold

In 1977 two spacecraft were launched on a journey into the cosmos.
They each carried a gold disc upon which was stored information
about Earth in the hope that should any alien life see it they would
know they are not alone.

Our message is not written
in gold to be collected by aliens

It is written
in autumn leaves for children to scatter

Our message is not written
in gold to die in the cosmos

It is written
in honey for bees to be born in

Our message is not written
in gold to be fought over by people

It is written
in daffodils so that friends can make peace

Our message is not written
in gold to be stored in quiet vaults

It is written
in the vocal cords for everyone to hear

Our message is not written
in gold to be aimed at by asteroids

It is written
in sand for the oceans to reach

Our message is not written
in gold to be lost in space

It is written
in candlelight for the lost to be found

Our message is not written
in gold to be forgotten by history

It is written
in rings to be remembered

Our message is not written
in gold to be swallowed by infinity

It is written
in the summer rain for the thirsty to drink

Our message is not written
in gold for spaceships to carry

It is written
in the sunrise for life to carry on

Dom

Oil

I've known you since nursery
when you picked me out of a dark corner
and chose me to be your friend.

We dug in the sandpit for treasure together,
uncovered the sweet fossils our mums
placed at the bottom of our birthday cakes.

We have discovered laughter in heartbreaks
and tears beneath the days which came
from blue skies.

Anger has cracked us but the ground
remains unbroken and each year
piles like sediment

the tiny moments of our friendship
layering onto older ones, deepening
our coastal shelf whilst oceans

wash over us.

They want to drill for oil in the Arctic,
tearing a million years of bedrock
to power a car.

I would not do this.
Our friendship is becoming a mountain.

Dom

The time my dog and I were stopped by a stranger

she said
Wo ist die Fähre?
?
but all I heard was the question mark
(and the sound of her eyes
trying to drop anchor).

A map, a finger
and the advice of footsteps
rushing to a distant bell
gave us the words
but only the smile
translated them.

Then my dog barked
and I explained we had to go.

Danke.
Dein Hund ist richtig schön.

Dom

22

Dog Years

Your voice low, you ask
how old Sally was
and I give her the dignity of dog years,
because seven is too close to you.

Yesterday I wished you aged
the other way
that years were months
and you and I could keep walking
through wonderlands
throwing worries into the distance
and forgetting where they land.

Tomorrow we will visit the beach
noticing the footprints of other dogs
mistaking them for lost photographs
and you will ask how old the dog was.
I won't tell you she was my age.

Dom

The receipt from the zoo gift shop

After we visited the zoo
we took home a stuffed lion
and the word 'brave'
and each night you'd fall asleep
holding both of them tight.

When you cried I gave you the lion
and called you brave
letting the stuffing gather your tears
and the word
dry them.

When you learned not to cry
I took away the lion
but left the word
imagining it would keep you safe
as it had me.

When you could not cry I gave you
my silence
as I searched for the receipt.

What a broken word 'brave' is.

A lion cries when it wants to.

Dom

We are not who we were

Though we are warmest in the womb
the chameleon climbs my arm
rejecting the fear to change

first leg second leg third leg fourth
exploring my body's stubborn branch
through chromatic reflections of now

without any thought of tomorrow
though the sun still waits, wondering
where he might choose to shed his colours.

Dom

Balance

Strength / Sun
Breathe / Breeze
Thrill / Thunder
Hike / Hill
Swim / Sea

Human / Nature

Dom

Underneath the City the Whale Swims

The whale swims underneath the city,
Deep down among the roots of steel and concrete,
Where pipes and cables wave like kelp.
Its low voice is held inside the groan of traffic.
Where neon splashes on the tarmac, you will see a ripple,
And you'll feel, in the small, salt pools of every cell,
The echo of its passing

Nicola

Even in the rain she'll be there,
   Spring through Summer into late
September, and always a Sunday,

taking care not to spoil her sari,
   unravelling her old ochre blanket
before kneeling on the grassy verge.

Her ritual begins with the weeding,
   moving on to pruning, trimming, digging,
turning the soil, sometimes planting,

most often in song, memoried from
   her mother's time – and ever so faintly –
so it most likely goes unheard unless

snatched by the breeze and whisked
   away for the ears of others. Only
occasionally will she break to sip

hot black tea from a flask until finally
  removing her gloves, nestling them
inside her basket, atop of the broccoli,

beans, potatoes, courgettes and more.
  Walking away now, she'll turn just once
to see her precious patch of earth.

James

Looking now at the poinsettia

The sun pushes her cart past our window
each day a little more stooped
each day in a little less time before
the crunch of stars is heard over the hill
but still, she manages to pull blues and yellows
from heartening soils whilst, as mother,
you get set to place a poinsettia on the sill.

You never wear lipstick or a dress to dance in
and your heart is a present without a label.
The sun sinks low and the ground turns white.
The poinsettia stays red.

Dom

Thanks to gravity, nothing ever
   escapes from this planet, except

perhaps the occasional rocket. No,
   nothing escapes and everything

gets renewed. *Like air*. Formed here,
   it remains here, forever refreshed by trees.

Like water. And wherever, whenever water
   began, it's survived the longest while;

so whatever you drink was once a pool
   where elephants go to cool; was once

a snowflake, briefly lodged in some
   Neanderthal's beard; and so too the arc

of the wave that first brought life to land.
   Like you. Yes you, young one, are impossibly

old, have been so many things, and will
   be all over again. So what to do?

Just carry on, being uniquely *you*.

                       James

Haiku from a Train

Florence railway station, August 2011

Who are these nightlings,
urbanites, risking their lives
working by starlight?

Onto drab concrete
they spray other-worldliness.
Coded messages.

Magic images:
golden monkeys, bears and fish.
The point of it is?

What matters is this:
alchemy of the city.
Viva graffiti!

James

The hug

Could you put your arms around a friend
as easily as you do a dog?
Mud-happy, autumn-free,
such greetings are open
unrestrained.

Whilst poetry cages love
that fur on skin, that tongue on face,
is how the sun greets the morning
the snow the mountain, the baby life.

I think I think too much
about what I hug
and how it fills tomorrow.

Dom

34

How to choose a pet

It was not easy
watching you walk from basket
to basket stroking, lifting, holding
each one in turn
then turning back to try again.

One was too timid
one not timid enough,
one was too spirited,
one whose tail did not wag
and another you thought
bore the sadness of all pets.

Each time I saw the weather within you
and wished I could make the decision for you
tell you this one's ears, this one's eyes, this one's
cry
would be the sort to make you feel loved
and this one's legs would run after you
when I could not.

But instead I watched and tried to decide
what sort of adult I wanted you to become.

Dom

Grandpa's Dogs

The dogs lay behind the pig pen door, as still as stones,
Until the squelch of Grandpa's boots across the yard
Set them barking, fit to bust.
He'd curse, and shout at them to hush,
Then tip the latch, when they'd fall silent,
And rush out, like always, fast, low slung and purposeful,
Intent as arrows, eager, as he was, to start the day.
High on the hill, they looked so separate, just specks
Spread out like planets, orbiting the green.
But they were one thing, my grandpa and his dogs,
Bound by sounds I was too far away to hear,
And love I was too young to understand.

Nicola

How to move like a rock

Rock is a sentence
with all its words removed
a silent conversation
(massively improved)
the song after its music
refuses to be grooved
the scientific theory
which cannot be disproved.

Rock is the centre
of a terrifying storm
the sudden screeching stop
when a car lets off its horn
the beating of a heart
when it's feeling all forlorn
the memories of parents
at the moment we are born.

Dom

Where Sunlight Sifts Cliff and Sky

The Book of British Birds

Huge and sacred, my 'Book of Kells',
the manuscript of my religion.
Small, proud pencil marks record
that I had seen a gannet by the age of ten
but not an Arctic skua,
a snipe, but not a water rail.

Those illustrations stamped my soul with icons
that still shine, and send me searching:
over ten miles of ankle-grabbing bog
for the silk grey and graphic pinstripe of a diver's throat;
tramping, frozen in a January dusk
to catch the dark bars of a woodcock's head.
Sometimes they catch me unawares,
when remembered image matches what I see.
And then I'm ten again
my heart huge,
bursting with the wonder of the sacred wild.

Nicola

*'The Reader's Digest Book of British Birds' was published in 1969.
Its stunning illustrations by the artist Raymond Harris-Ching
influenced a whole generation of naturalists.*

Every night she would dream
  of wings; watching, touching, even
growing wings: the lucid, amber wings

of dragonflies or bees; the dusted,
  flimsy wings of moths; the so-white
wings of angels; the veined and leathery

wings of bats; of course, the wings
of birds: of doves, of owls and starlings –
with all their feathers, *feathers*;

and each and every night, wings
  stretching, tensing, readying,
for her own life of flight to come.

                              James

Why Humans?

In the tangerine sky above the station,
the starlings are doing 3D modelling.
Their telepathic computation
makes ten thousand bodies code for density and form:
A perfect sphere, then curtains in the wind;
A whale that leaps and turns into a swan
whose wings spread out into a waterfall,
which cascades in waves and waves,
that break above the rain-glazed rooftops,
into formless scatter, mere bird matrix;
till a new flock-thought plot
causes them to climb and climb and twine,
into a vast, fat rope of bodies,
curled to make a giant question mark.
A massive why hangs for a moment above the city,
before, like reverse smoke,
the flock's sucked down
to roost inside the dark horizon.

Nicola

43

Finch

He taught me all the names for finch:
goldfinch, bullfinch, greenfinch, rose finch,
but also canary, linnet, redpoll, grosbeak,
summer sun, morning meadow, ripening wheat.
He taught me the word for waking and hearing her
in the garden, picking blackberries,
hanging the washing, telling the day
there will be food and a breeze
and oh how his eyes would sing
when she flew to us.

Dom

Peregrine

Where sunlight sifts cliff and sky
to one white shaft,
A peregrine distils out of the world's wildness.
It flies along the very edge of possibility.
Mayhem spurts
Where its path has sliced open the neat guts of physics.
It stoops into the sea's roar,
Recruiting gravity to fund more speed.
It's lost in foam-flames, fume, then up,
A fierce, dark comet,
Burning back into the blue.

Nicola

Swift by your Side

Circle as you sleep, my love
and drift upon your dreams.
Ruling from the clouds, my love
is simpler than it seems.

Be queen above the world, my love
be the king who's free to fly.
Let the wealth within your wings, my love
be scattered in the sky.

The kingdom of your eye, my love
is measured by the sun.
The journey to my heart, my love
begins when that is done.

I hear your piper's call, my love
the poetry of tears.
I'll follow where you lead, my love
as months turn into years.

And when we go to ground, my love
when all our wings are old.
We'll gaze up to the blue, my love
and count our words of gold.

Dom

Crow

Come, Crow – bring down the night.
Spread wide those scraggy, wizened wings.
Swoop low. Dive deep. Take flight.

With sharpened beak, peck out the stars,
each one by one from charcoal sky.
And from that mind of soot and scars

work your crafty charms of old
and send whole cities off to sleep
then leave us blind and cold.

Drum up shadows, dusty ghosts,
and those that dwell in dark.
Free their ancient, broken souls.

Swap moon for sun then go.
The day is dead. Your work is done.
The night has come, old Crow.

James

Isn't it incredible

that a creature
that seems
as unremarkable
as you little skylark

can not only
propel itself
into the heavens

but also
plummet
back to earth
like some
feathery
pebble

and all
the while
singing
that sweet
fuzzy warble
of a song

one so joyful
and so utterly
Spring-zinged

it's as
if you're
informing
the world
that you've
just invented
sunshine

James

Motorway Cinquain

Here comes

speckle-feather,

soaring high, swooping low,

beneath a blue-black sea of night.

Old owl.

James

Listen to the one who doesn't write poetry

I'm asking who does the owl turn to
after hooting out his advice
on summer nights whilst I
lie in bed dreading the morning.

He knows everything and nothing
in the way all those sorts of people
who talk too much and listen too little
make an echo from one wise word.

But he knows enough to understand
when to let the quiet air carry him.

Dom

Manx Shearwater

Off Cabo Norte,
Off Punta Jericoacoara,
Or Calanhar and Mar Chiquita, Punta Sur.
In the twilight,
Where the phosphorescence dots the long Atlantic swells,
A bird, brown and small,
Holds inside her head, six thousand miles of sea
And the rooty darkness of the Skomer burrow
Where all her journeys hinge.
There, the chick she was, the chick she makes
Peeps and peeps,
Fluffy-fat and ready for the miles and miles
For the phosphorescence and the twilight
For the long Atlantic swells,
Off Cabo Norte,
Off Punta Jericoacoara,
Or Calanhar and Mar Chiquita, Punta Sur.

Nicola

Gannets

A gannet's eyes are bluest blue,
Not baby blue, but blue of ice.
There is no warmth inside that hue,
A gannet's nature is not 'nice'!
Their beaks are swords, they use to stab
Nest neighbours in the colony;
Their homes are spaced by range of jab,
That's gannet city geometry.
But maybe when you get your dinner
By smashing head first in the sea,
'Niceness' isn't such a winner
And what you need's ferocity.
If from ninety feet you had to dive
How fierce you'd be, just to survive!

Nicola

Choughs at Marloes

Kiaow! Kiaow!
The choughs are coming.
Their black silk fingertips
Tickle the updraught
So it smiles them into flight.

They slide,
A hand's breadth from the clifftop
Then, down, as if the sunwarmed turf
had just come up to kiss them.

They gleam,
They glint, slick black,
Their bud-red beaks bright against the green,
Busy blustering beetles from their holes.

Kiaow! Kiaow!
Their voices strike the glass-still air,
Making it chime and chime,
Ringing in the Springtime.
CHOUGHS

Nicola

Swan

Moon-bright, heart-light
I wish your wings upon the world
Each time I come to watch
Your feathers unfurl the snow's flag
From Winter's wind.

Tree-tired, bough-heavy
I take your wings upon my back
When I remember you remember nothing
Except how Spring will skip in waves
Over dark water.

Dom

Feral Canada Geese

At home they would be flying South.
Fleeing the first snow flurries,
riding on the Autumn gales.
They wouldn't be alone;
there would be skeins of cranes
slow-flapping, with their cronk-croak cries
and busy vees of smaller waterfowl and waders.
The sky would be written all over with birds,
knowing where where they're going, purposeful, determined.
But here, there's no migration and no purpose,
no skeins of cranes, or ducks or waders.
No ice, or snow or peril.
There's just the flooded field beside the sewage works
and a man and dog, who look up
as the geese flap in uneasy circles.

Nicola

Without a name

a goose is still a goose; it's no more
or less goosey for having one.

And most likely it couldn't give
a honk what it's called. So too
the flamingo, the kookaburra

and the weeny hummingbird.
Nothing actually wants a name,
asks for a name, and yet we have

to hand them out or otherwise
we'd be forever saying, 'Hey!'
'What?' 'Look!' 'Where?' 'There!'

'At what?' 'That airborne, feathery *thing*!'
'Which one?' 'That one – right *there*!'
Which wouldn't do. Surely someone

somewhere owns a copy of *The Bumper
Book of Brand New Birdie Names*,
all ready to dish out fresh offerings

like 'tweetie-beak', 'swamp-duck',
'pinkie-puff' or the glorious
'purple-plumed dooble-snuffer' –

which would no doubt make
even the hissiest, huffiest,
fussiest goose quite jealous.

James

The Nest

On
a walk
through a wood
I find it
on the ground.

Light,
like a hat;
round,
like a crown.

Built
through the spring
through the wind
through the rain
as a home
where life
could begin
again –

from
somewhere up
in the trees
above,
and now
in my hand,
this weave of love.

James

Bird and Boy

Two twigged feet pitch a fat green tent
upon the wheelchair's arm
and a moment forms a clearing
as a wing's well-worn map folds down.

This precipice of calloused leather
is where boy and bird meet daily
to discuss the slowdown of heartbeats
in the wordless language of friends

which holds as steady as a tardigrade
against the hurricane of a hand.
Prod. Push. Poke. He tests the bird's resolve
but tremors cannot tear the two apart

even when the heartbeat stops
and the boy moves far away.
A sudden creased crumple of feathers
and the bird decamps.

Dom

The Deep, Deep Blue

Ammonite

The Winter storms have washed up a wonder:
A coil of shell curls in your hand,
So perfect that it looks alive.

And yet, it's not.
The shell is stone,
The creature that once lived inside,
Long turned to dust.

But for a moment
As you hold this little fossil in your hand
You can be with it, swimming in an ancient sea.

Nicola

Just One Place

If I could give you just one place,
It would be this:
The see-through blue of ocean shallows,
The crinkle-gleam of rippled light;
The not-quite-turquoise tint of waves before they break;
The voice of surf;
The continents of flimsy foam, that float and fade,
Breaking, coalescing, drifting,
To tell the fleeting histories of land.
'Only this endures,' they seem to say,
'Water, light and sand.'

Nicola

Paddling

I wanted to be water
to wrap my arms around the planet
and hold the memory of everything
that's ever lived

to feel the beat of hearts
which never met
to hear the words
which fell short of ears

and I would be everywhere at once
even breathing air into the sky
saying I am here
when the tide goes out.

Dom

The Pond

Now it seems
like a dream
that June afternoon
when we found
the pond
by the path.

And the pond
was alive, brimful,
bristling, wriggling
with brand-new life.

And you cupped
your hands,
skimmed through
the water,
as one little tickler
twitched in your palm;
just a blob for a body
and a pointy tail,
so black, like soot,
like a miniature whale:
such a restless soul
is a tadpole.

James

*R*arely a day passes
when *i* don't walk beside you –
delighting in your ne*V*er-ending, winding,
w*e*nding, slow-meander
stream-of-chatte*r*

James

The Bucket

Do you remember
that afternoon, dashing
across the sand? Bucket
in hand, net in the other,
then hovering over
every pool? And once
we'd done, hurrying back,
bucket now full, everyone
trying to catch a glimpse
of two little fish,
three green crabs,
and all of those
fidgety shrimps?

Then finally strolling
back to sea, wading out,
T-shirts wet, tipping
them into the waves?

How could we
ever forget?

James

Limpet

Limpet, is it simple
living in the dimple
of the patch, the mark, the pock
that your shell makes on the rock?
When the tide's out, there you hunker
like a soldier in a bunker,
while your muscly sucker foot
keeps you stuck down like a root,
Until the waves rise, and your grasp
is loosed, so you can rasp
at the coating scum of weed,
as you wander off to feed,
with antennae and a trail,
demonstrating you're a snail.
Now the tide is on the turn,
to your spot you must return,
where your shell fits to the rock
like a key within a lock.
Tides and years roll on, roll round
but, always, here you're found:
Limpet, simple
in your dimple.

Nicola

Lantern Fishes

Sailors squinting at their sonar screens
Thought it was a secret weapon,
A fiendish plot to make them think
the sea floor had moved upwards.

It was a secret, just one of many that the ocean keeps –
Like where blue whales have their babies
Or how long sunfish live –
But this one was bigger,
Vast in fact, huge, enormous, everywhere:
A layer moving from the depths of every ocean, every night,
And sinking with the dawn.
A phenomenon as big as tides or sunrise.
Even now we know just what it is,
It's still mysterious.
It is the biggest movement on the planet,
A mass, mass, mass migration of little fish,
Too shaped by deep to survive where we can see them;
In our world, they exist in jars,
Pickled on museum shelves
Deader than a tinned sardine.
Yet, in the twilight zone,
They are star-studded galaxies,
Whose slow gyrations
Shape our world as surely as the sun and moon.

Nicola

Lantern fish are the most numerous vertebrates on the planet. Every night countless billions of them migrate from deep waters, and come closer to the surface to feed, then return at dawn, depositing millions of megatonnes of carbon onto the sea floor in their poo. Their effect on our atmosphere and climate is huge and only just starting to be understood.

Night-Time Reef

It's like walking through a town at 2 a.m.
Almost everyone's in bed asleep and
anyone you meet looks surprised or guilty.
The city-centre crowds of plankton feeding fish have gone,
the busy shoppers foraging between the coral heads
are absent too.
Eels slurp about like furtive drunks
and sharks shy away like burglars from a cop car.
It's only when you switch your torch off that you see the action:
exploding stars of tiny bioluminescent things,
dots of neon in a black so deep you lose all sense of scale;
You could be spectating galaxies
initiating supernovae with your little finger.

Nicola

The Emperor's Ice

Winter's creeping back.
The sea is turning into ice.
At first just spikes and spicules,
like thorns of glass tangling the water.
Then, pans and pancakes filling up the bays,
wobbling with winds and waves;
as the sun sinks for a season, they set to solid,
locked to land, held fast by freezing.
Ice forms a big blank page,
twice the size of Canada,
from which all life retreats.
All life, save these:
whose shadows the last, low light casts, long,
like lines of text announcing
to the passing satellite,
that the Emperors have once more come to claim their kingdom.

Nicola

Narwhal Sonnet

The deep, deep blue between the floes
Is split with backs like marbled stone.
The air rings with their breathy blows,
The clatter-clash of bone on bone.
They joust and parry, feint and lunge,
Each lance a spiral tooth that's six feet long,
Then, down into the depths they plunge
To feast below, now all the fighting's done.
The Vikings traded narwhal tusks for gold,
Every Prince and King in Europe had their horn;
Each one was magic, that's the tale the Vikings told,
And came not from a whale, but from a Unicorn.
If Unicorns are myth and narwhals real,
Why is it narwhal magic that I feel?

Nicola

Greenland Shark

Ancient tree of the sea,
will you answer me?
Unknot me some wisdom
from your hundred years and more
of rooting your migrations
to the sunken paths of continents.

Teach me
the slow ways.

Ancient tree of the sea,
turn my life like a leaf in the wind.
Let me drift in the light of moon,
whispering to the children
who will stand ankle-deep
in the Arctic tide.

Guide me
through the currents.

Ancient tree of the sea,
chart the dark rocks of my heart
and break them into soil
for a future to grow in.
You are the pulse
of the world.

Show me
how to swim.

Dom

52 Blue – The Loneliest Whale

He's a high-pitched singer
crystal ringer
dancing on his own
like a lone gunslinger
firing out beats
of water notation
spinning his song
to his own rotation.

Big and wide
rocking side to side
taking his groove
out for a ride.
A musical ocean
lends the notion
of swimming the depths
in a blissed-out motion

He's a mover a groover
a big shrimp hoover
chewing on tunes
guaranteed to move her
setting the pace
to a lumbering grace
always a sun-happy
smile on his face.

52 Blue.
Unique not new.
Dancing to the word
that can't be heard.
52 Blue
52 Blue
Dancing for himself
Not me or you.

Dom

Note: 52 Blue is the name of a single whale who sings at a higher frequency than any other whale on Earth. That means none of the other whales can hear or answer him.

Cerulean

when Whale dipped out of sight
pulling away from a kiss with God
and swapping sky for sea
it left behind a reminder
in the blue used to clothe summer
and feather the kingfisher
a reminder pigmented in memories
to say breathing isn't a privilege of above
nor the sea a prison for below

Dom

Which creature would you be?

Today I'd choose a whale. We all need
to roam and there's no greater space

than an ocean. A galaxy of salt water
right here on earth. And who wouldn't
want to be that huge hulk of life? To see

in sound, to talk in song, to cruise the blue
or lose yourself in endless days of play:
lurching skywards, flopping backwards,

ever huffing lung-loads of warm air
back into the world? Tell me then:
which other beast is as wise

as the moon, has the heart of a star –
or a belly full of memories
from way back when?

James

For National Poetry Day 2021, on the theme of 'Choices'.

Green Song

Green Song

Rain will fall and wind will blow
Plant the seed and let it grow
The sun will dance her daily round
To sing your seed out of the ground.

Green the shoot and green the leaf
Sky above and earth beneath
When green is held beneath your hand
Life will once more own the land.

Inside the seed a forest sings
In rustling leaves and beating wings
A wild green pulse that calls in rhyme
Linking life across all time.

Hand and root and heart and seed
Nature gives us all we need
We are of one kin, you and me,
The bird, the beetle, and the tree
The bird, the beetle, and the tree.

Nicola

It's Not Hard to Make a Forest

A seed.
A bird.
A bird, a seed.
A seed and bird.
Again.
Again, again.
A seed.
Some rain.
A seed.
Some sun.
A seed.
Some time.
A root, a shoot, a leaf.
A tree?
A tree!
A seed.
A bird.
Again, again, again.

Nicola

Seasons 4

AUTUMN's a breeze
that sneaks 'round trees
and tickles them till
they lose their leaves.

WINTER's a gust
of huffs and puffs –
the gifts it gives are
sniffs and coughs.

SPRING's a tweet
a pulse a beat
a dance to lift our
hearts and feet.

SUMMER's a hoot
and hot that's what
a chance to do
well not a lot!

James

The Tree Whale

The Tree Whale crashed here long ago
when forests ceased their wooden flow.
She beached upon the grassy hill,
and then for aeons lay quite still.

She used to soar, she used to swim
where sunbeams spill upon the rim
of chestnut leaves and oaken crowns –
where eagles issued regal sounds.

She used to see the clouds curl round
a distant sky, where lands are found –
where Ancients sang of times gone by,
before the smog bricked up the sky.

Now, overgrown with chanterelles
she hatches plans in dappled dells,
from where she nurtures baby seeds
in mossy nests with thorny weeds.

Where, after time, two tender stalks
will stretch and spread like timid hawks
to rise and wave above the whale

until they bloom . . . and then set sail.

Now Tree Whale, through one bleary eye,
will watch her children wave goodbye.
she knows all things must change or end –
but has one hope:

remain their friend.

Dom

A tree
is not like you and
me – it waits around quite
patiently – catching kites and
dropping leaves – reaching out to touch
the breeze . . . A tree all day will stand and stare
clothed in summer, winter : bare – it has no shame
or modesty . . . Perhaps its generosity is the greatest in
the world – it gives a home to every bird, every squirrel,
feeds them too – to every dog it is a loo . . . And after dark
what does it do? Catch a falling star or two? Shimmy
in the old moonlight? Or maybe have a conker fight?
A tree can give an awful lot : the wood to make a
baby's cot – pencils, paper, tables, chairs – lolly
sticks as well as stairs . . . Without a tree we
could not live – a tree, it seems just
loves to give –
but us :
we
chop
we
take
we
burn
that's
what we
do in return.

James

They wouldn't le*T* you near it now.

Too wild t*h*ey'd say. Yet

we were there, nearly *e*very day.

In that w*O*od, we were

the wild ones, free to *l*ive. Free to get lost.

And we *d*id.

We built a den. *We* leapt over streams.

We sat in the chattering trees. *Or* made maps, or set traps

or fought the invading Vikings. *One* rule, hard and fast:

we had to be home by *d*ark.

James

Grass Dance

Grass, GRASS.
I mean

wow

lining the hillside
like a billion green arms
waving in the wind
swaying to a song
only they can hear.

Put your ear there.
Swing to the beat there.
Try to squeeze between
the crowd there

and wait until dawn
when they stand
silver lights raised high
looking at the sun
with tears in their eyes.

Dom

Hay Making

So full of yellow sunshine,
Warm as fresh custard,
The meadow looks good enough to eat.
I'll plunge in my spoon,
Through the frosting of flowers,
Pink and white and yellow,
Delicate as ice cream,
Through the crunchy layer of seed heads,
Grasses, docks and plantain
To the juicy bite of stalks and leaf blades
Studded with crickets and beetles, like dried fruit.
Right down into the roots and soil,
Moist and dark, chewy, rich and spicy.
I won't stop until it's all gone
Until I'm full of it –
Grass, and flowers,
Beetles, crickets, sunshine,
Full to bursting,
Like the barn,
Full of new-made hay.

Nicola

*'. . . take only pictures,
leave only footprints . . .'*

Whenever you walk
beyond the town

by rivers, in woods
where all around

live truly wildly
please step lightly

act so wisely
always kindly

James

Plant an Acorn Now to Give
Your Grandchildren Shade

There will always still be sky.

No matter what happens, you'll look up and see the blue,
Maybe you'll remember that butterfly
On the yellow flower, and the nettle sting that made you cry.
It will be long ago by then, and flowers might be few
But there will always still be sky.
Remembering's important. Every day I try
To remember something. Today it was a cuckoo
I once saw, its beak wide open to let out its cry;
It was so close, I looked right in its eye.
Sometimes remembering hurts. Then what gets me through
Is that there will always still be sky.
There are other things too. Today I saw a greenfly
Like a speck of paint with wings. It landed on my shoe.
We used to use a spray to kill them. I don't know why.
Back then we used to make all insects die
But that was back before, before we had to say it, before we knew,
There will always still be sky
There will always still be sky.

Nicola

101

What Will You Remember When You Are Old?

They look up at you with big eyes
and ask for a creature from the Time Before,
distant and unreal to them as tap water.
A memory is what they want
of something huge and vivid,
alive with its un-human stink
and slow, slow breath that you could feel with your eyes closed.

But you have nothing.
No whale blow, resonant as a concert hall,
No elephant's trunk, reaching with precise tenderness.
No giraffe, impossibly long limbed, loping through a golden dusk.
Not even the sudden flick of a starling's wing,
A glimpse of fox's eye-shine in the dark,
A slither-jump of startled froglet.

All you have is the swipe, swipe, swipe,
that you learned first and most, of all things,
and the bright little rectangle, that your mind grew to fit.
It fitted you for nothing in that world,
or in this one,
where children squat in the grime
and rub their bony knuckles to their eyes
in astonishment at what you failed to see.

Nicola

Animal Alphabet

A should always be for aardvark,
Axolotl, aye-aye, avocet and asp,
Not android and acrylic, accelerometer and app.

I don't want B to be for bitcoin, binary or barcode
But for bear and boar and binturong,
Beaver, barracuda, bison, bandicoot and bass.

C can't stand for client, code and content,
Nor for the post-apocalyptic cockroach.
I want it still to be for caracal and capybara,
Cougar, cuttlefish, coati, cuscus and cockatoo.

And D for DOS? And debug? Digital?
No! No, D's for dotterel and dunlin,
Dik-dik, dhole and dugong,
Dace and drongo, dragonet.

What I fear, is that we'll lose the letters
All the way from addax to zorilla.
That all we'll have is E,
Not for earwig, eel and emu
Nor echidna, eland, elk
But for that other E entirely,
The end eternal, that's Extinct.

Nicola

Who cares

if we poison the land,
the seas? We fell all the forests,
we topple the trees? There's plenty
more galaxies, planets like these — with
water, with air, with warmth, with light:
homes like ours just right for life. Who cares
if we lose those buzzy old bees? Who cares
if there's plastic clogging the seas? When
our blue world is finally done, we'll leave
this rock and mother sun, we'll zoom
on up — to way out where — there's
many more earths . . .
or are there?

James

For National Poetry Day 2019, on the theme of 'Truth'.

A Song for the Future, a Song for the Past

Remember the day when we killed the bees,
and we sent the whales to an early grave?
Remember the ice melting in the seas,
and how we burned the trees we would not save?

We said our hands were tied, that rules were rules –
said we'd record the songs that nature played.
We said trust our wisdom, we need the tools
to build a world that will not fade.

Science will save us, take us to the stars,
find a whole new world, be our Noah's Ark.
Perhaps if we lived on a cold, dead Mars
then the future we face would make its mark.

Write your obituaries whilst you may.
Let words shock the world into life today.

Dom

When

When London's under twenty feet of sea
And it takes a four-hour queue to get a dinner.
When you dream of biscuits and of tea,
The way you used to dream of being a lottery winner.

When you can't remember when you last brushed your teeth,
Or how it felt to flick a switch for light.
When your whole life feels just like funeral wreath,
And you fear your youngest may not make it through the night.

You'll wonder what the hell we were all doing
To let the whole world get in such a state
And look for those who brought us to this ruin
And failed to act before it was too late.

They'll be right there, those old climate change deniers,
Roasting rats beside you over bomb site fires.

Nicola

Rude Boys Rinsed

A climate change sonnet for William Shakespeare

We've used this planet like a jakes,
And filled its sweet blue welkin with our dross,
Until the whole world now with ague shakes,
And every day another creature cries its loss.
We pleach our hearts with greed, our ears enclog,
Beshrew the truth of science shouting loud
And shuffle on, so many clotpoles in a fog,
Our eyes tight shut against the coming cloud.
We're ruled by coxcombs, popinjays and twits,
Who'd swallow up a universe to save their skins;
They care for nothing but the gold that stuffs their scrips,
And can't see that here's a game that no one wins.
Wake up blood, there ain't no time to wait,
Rude boys rinsed, now eco-warriors the bait!

Nicola

A 'jakes' is a toilet; the 'welkin' is the sky above; an 'ague' is a fever; to 'pleach' is to fold; to 'beshrew' is to denounce; 'clotpoles', 'coxcombs' and 'popinjays' are varieties of numbskull; a 'scrip' is a wallet.

Can There Be Sky?

Can there be a Spring
if the swallow doesn't bring it?
Can there be a song
if the robin doesn't sing it?
Can a heart be light
With no sparrow's chirp to raise it?
Can a sky be blue
With no singing lark to praise it?
What will our world be
With no birds or beasts to share it?
Alone upon the earth?
We could never bear it!

Nicola

Tomorrow, Today

Dire warnings, melting icecaps, giant storms and failing crops.
Dire warnings, droughts and heatwaves, forest fires and empty
    shops.
It's a never-ending chorus of misery and gloom,
Enough to make you stop your ears and never leave your room.
But just supposing for a minute we got it right instead of wrong,
Then the future could be singing a very different kind of song.
Cities without traffic noise, and air that's safe and clean.
City farms that grow your food and streets all lined with green.
No slaughterhouses dealing out the blood and death and sorrow,
A Petri dish is where you'll get the bacon of tomorrow.
You won't need to get tangled in the getting-spending snare,
Your wealth won't be in money but in what you've learned to
    share.
'Growth' won't mean roads and factories, but coral reefs and trees,
And eco-system healing will be our GDP.
The future will be built upon the choices that you made,
So plant an acorn now to give your grandchildren some shade.

Nicola

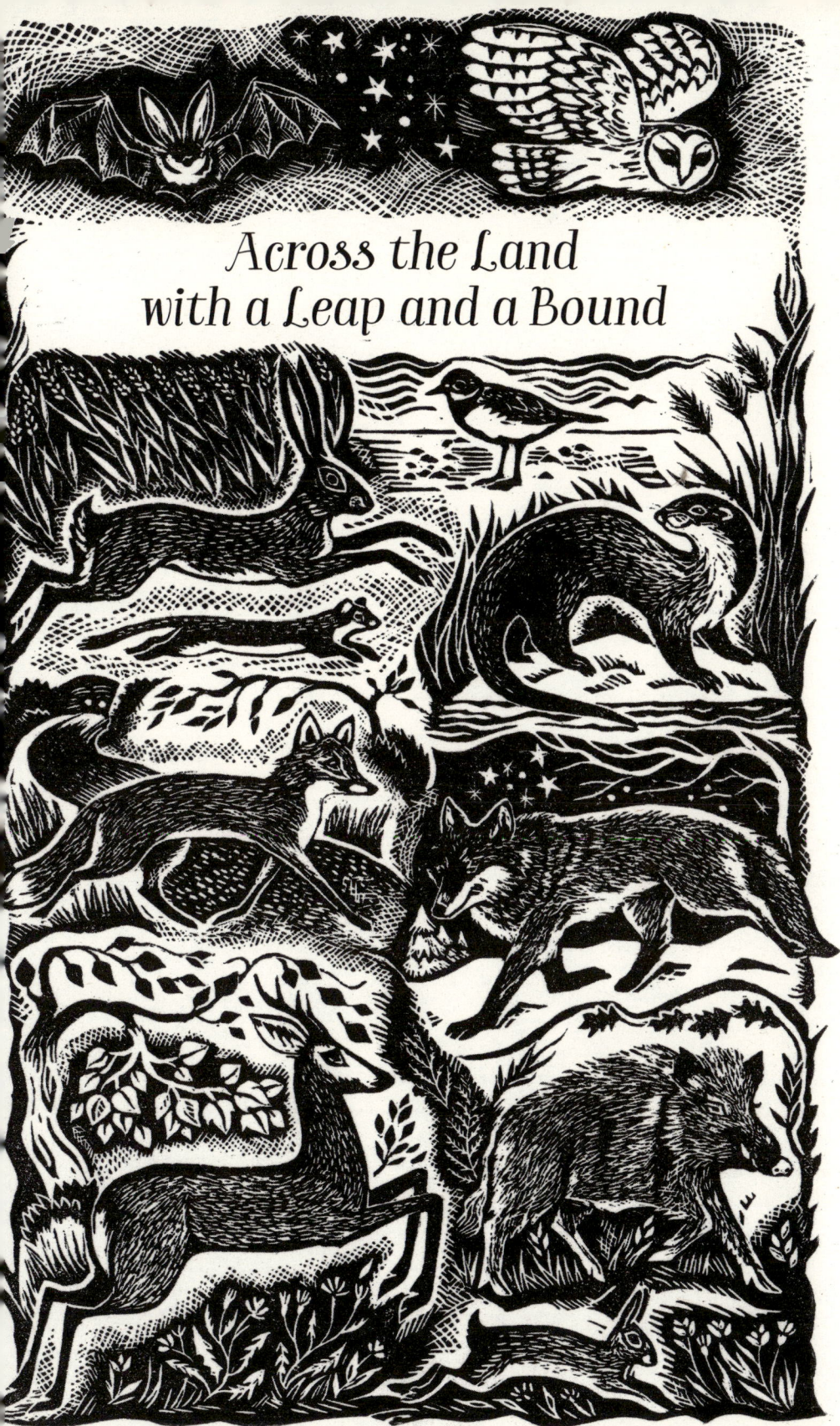

Across the Land
with a Leap and a Bound

Still

Be still!
Still as the brindled leveret
between the grass stalks.
Still as the spotted fawn
in the dappled shade.
Still as the ringed plover
amongst the weedy shingle.

Drop from the world's eye,
Vanish from its ears, its nose, its tongue.
Be untasted, undetected, un-divined.
Unspoken.
Un-noticed.
Be still enough to see
the shiver zone of light and shadow
the boundary of sound and silence
the place where leverets and fawns hold still,
and you are not reflected in the plover's eye.

Nicola

Mountain Hare

Maukin, maigheach-gheal, mountain hare
the shape winter takes in spring
melting into the cracks
where the cold still clings,
the leap from the lea
ahead of the fox's shadow
as fire chases ice,
the mittened fist
hiding the surprise
of snow.

Dom

Somewhere out there is that hare.
   Has to be. Saw it last week. Just over
the road, beyond the barn, amidst the gold

of the corn field. Thought it was a rabbit;
   then we clocked those ears, and woah,
did that flatfoot go. So swift! Across

the land with a leap and a bound,
   like its cousin could only dream of.
So we'll wait till late to head out there,

to glimpse that whiskery whizz of a hare,
   that non-stop nomad, dweller of nowhere –
but absolutely *anywhere* . . .

James

The Sun and the Hare

When Sun was young
he rode the Earth on Hare's back.
Hot as thoughtlessness
he burned and Hare bucked and leaped,
crossing mountains and myths,
ice ages and oceans until,
jealous of a volcano, Sun eased
into the foothills, dismounted, and
was about to drink the land dry
when he noticed Hare's brown fur
glowing golden. Angry, but unable
to become incandescent, he tried
to reclaim what he thought was his.
But Hare was too fast,
slipping away like Sun's youth.

Dom

Fox, what have you done?
    You should have slipped away by now.
Look. Here comes the sun. Did you

not spot those blazing lights, or hear
    the engine's rage? Surely you must
know by now a road is never safe?

So here you are, on your side,
    your eyes are blinkless, newly-blind;
your coat's still regal, rusty-red:

immaculate you are in death.
      You've left this world.
   Next life, beware. Next time you're
on the night shift, please take care.

James

Batswoopswoop

You're a rag, a bag
a game of tag
looping swooping
snatching swag

You're the shadow of a flame
in a quick-fire game
the heart of a hero's
comic-book fame

Batswoopswoop batswoopswoop
Doing air dances till you droop

You're a skater, a baiter
a stay-out-later
flying the sky like
a will-not-wait-er

You're the blink of an eye
in a stormy sky
the always-miss
and will-not-die

Batswoopswoop batswoopswoop
Doing air dances till you droop

You're a crack, a smack
a lightning thwack
the everywhere kid
who's got my back

You're alive, a jive
a big high five
flitting not sitting
to a soar-and-dive

Batswoopswoop batswoopswoop
Doing air dances till you droop
Batswoopswoop batswoopswoop
Doing air dances till you droop

Dom

I'm Beastly, Me

Once I've **WOLF**ed
my supper down,
I'm **SLUG**ish
so I **SLOTH** around.

I have to **CAT** nap,
or I'm **RAT**ty,
so **DOG**-tired
I get all **CRAB**by.

You won't **BEAR** it
if I snore.
And I ain't **LION**,
it's a **BOAR**.

Ooh deary **DEER**,
I **RABBIT** on.
I'm **HORSE** from
YAKking far too long.

Now **OWL** be gone,
for I c**ANT** stop.
I've got to **FLY**
so I'll **BEE** off . . . !

James

If you've ever seen a wolf

in the wild – or so the old
saying goes – it's seen you

a thousand times before.
So maybe the same is true
of a mouse. Think of whenever

you've been alone and made
the most of that moment:
you've sung so loud; invented

a dance; bounced on your bed
like a kangaroo. And once, just
once – you may have discovered

that you had been watched
by a mouse: apricot-brown,
with two unflinching, ebony eyes.

So what to do? Nothing.
Be good to your whiskery
neighbour: it will not judge,

nor laugh at you, nor grade
    your dance out of 5. Just let
it return to the world below,

knowing your home
    is no longer
your own.

James

She watches the world
through star-gold eyes:

with awe but mostly
suspicion; she'll sniff

at the air, she'll wait,
she'll listen, she'll sense

the slightest footfall;
she'll skulk through the night

in her old winter coat
beneath an ocean of sky;

she'll leap over snow
with limbs as fleet

as the wind's invisible wings;
she'll follow the promise

of even the wisp
of a meal.

Here in my dreams,
those darkest woods,

nothing bewitches me
more than her:

that great grey wolf.

James

Come On Out,
you web-of-foot,
you claw-of-hand,
you wiz-in-water,
born-of-land;
you rascal,
weasel,
river-slither,
wet-of-coat and
white-of-whisker;
I know you're there
you quicksilver,
undulator,
duck 'n' diver,
ripple-maker;
nip-'n'-nifty,
super-slinky,
what-a-rotter —
oh, I'll spot you
one day,
otter . . . !

James

128

My First Badger

We both had our minds on other things:
Mine, on my mother's voice
and the shame of being homesick
when I'd fought so hard to leave;
His, on his empty belly
and the scarcity of worms in this dry Summer.
Wildlife programmes talked of stealth and silence,
but he made so much noise!
I heard him long before I saw him,
scrunching vegetation and gruntily complaining
about the hardness of the ground.
He pushed through to where I sat,
tucked in the hedge, crying,
his scarred, old snout so close to the earth,
his grumbling so loud,
that he did not notice me until he walked into my shins!
For ten long seconds we looked at each other,
me and the badger.
I took in the subtle curve of his snout,
the way his stripes fitted to his head, his neat ears,
the dark-spark eyes that made no sense of me.
Then, he turned and ran, his bottom wobbling in retreat.
My tears dried.
I remembered crocodiles and leopards,
macaws and gibbons, giant anteaters,
and all the far-off things that I was going to see!

Nicola

Home is Wherever
Your Spirit is Free

Gorilla Gazing

London Zoo, Easter 2008

He sits and he stares
with those old brown eyes
beyond the glass
beyond my gaze
to a time
and a place
he's never known
yet somehow
seems to remember

Where the wind
shakes the trees
where the rain
wets the leaves
where there are
no walls at all

He sits and he stares
like an ancient sage
beyond the glass
beyond my gaze
to a world
long gone
and wonders why
we're all
so far
from home

James

Yes, it was the Romans who
first brought elephants to Britain, or *Britannia*
as they had chosen to name it. Loads of them.
They probably thought they'd impress those early
Brits with their herds of loveable lumpies. But
it was actually the circus that brought this one
particular elephant to town – to London, that
is, or *Londinium,* as the Romans had decided
to call it. There was a photo in the newspaper
the very next day – of a full-size, African
elephant there in the circus arena, somehow
managing to step so lightly in between
each of the five men lying on a rug
in the ring. Thank goodness too, as
one of them happened to be my dad.

James

The Monkey and the Apple
Whipsnade Zoo, Summer 2012

Monkey doesn't seem to notice
   the rain or even the noisy tourists
for his mind is on the apple

left over from feeding time,
   the red one that bobs half-afloat
on the surface of the little lake.

After several moments of head-slapping
   and chin-scratching, Monkey disappears,
returning with the twiggiest of sticks

to prod the apple, over and again,
   attempting to bring it back to shore.
Admitting defeat, he chucks his tool

onto the water and it's only then
   that he greets his audience, graces
them with a 'whatever' gaze, an almost

'you get it, if you're that smart' sneer,
   before scrambling off into the late
afternoon of the trees.

James

Elephant

Where on earth
would you begin
to paint an elephant?

That quick-witted,
ocean-memoried,
grey hunk of a thing?

Linking
tail-to-trunk
to tail-to-trunk,
over the
dusty plains?

Marching through
the clatter
of some Summer
street parade?

Or alone
out there
in the starry dark,
turning over
the cold bones
of one long gone?

And what would
you paint it with?

Colours
or words?

James

Elephant Smile

It turns out
you won

well done

my inch-thick skin
perfect (I thought)
for weathering sandstorms,
the sun's relentless gaze,
and grief
was no match for your
high-calibre bullet.

And that was that.

Sixty plus years of guiding my family
across a continent
ended.

The worth of me
divided

into ivory
and a photo of us.

Dom

Giraffe

The first time she saw
that Baba Yaga of bony straw

she checked the grass,
the sky, the gravity and air

to be sure she hadn't stepped
onto another planet where

more earthly hands would not
drag those who sought to soar,

where the sky was just
another open door.

Dom

Home is wherever your spirit
   is free. And so for me, it's here; where
snow is ever my constant companion,

moreover my name. Where maverick
   winds numb these winter-white whiskers,
cut beneath my speckled coat, chill

my bones and the breath of my lungs
   and darken my inner world. There's such
little air yet more pale sky than clouds

could ever hope for. This solitude isn't
   just refuge, but starlight for my soul;
makes me the creature I am. And so,

have you guessed I am snow leopard?
   A lone and living ghost, at the most
only a leap beyond your human eye.

Forged from ancient and mighty stone:
   my mountain, my wilderness,
my universe, my home.

                                        James

How Many Minibeasts?

How Many Minibeasts?

A *stampede* of millipedes?
A *festival* of fleas?
An *earful* of earwigs?
A *business* of bees?

A *rock 'n' roll* of dung beetles?
A *squadron* of wasps?
A *scuttling* of ladybugs?
A *discotheque* of moths?

A *fidgeting* of earthworms?
A *nastiness* of nits?
A *beastliness* of minibeasts?
This poem makes me *ITCH*!

James

Sugar the bee and me

A honey-warm day and she carries me
cool bed to warm grass
beside a bee.

Then a shade for me and a book for me and
nothing for me to do except
watch the bee

curled like a fist around a gold coin
gathering strength
like me.

We do not give sugar to the bee
and so I will not ask her to carry me.

Dom

September Haiku

The white butterfly
takes sips of sugar water
from my open hand

having just survived
the cruelty of the cat's paw
mere moments ago

before flittering
into the welcoming arms
of the walnut tree

James

The Holy Rollers

The Romans and the Ancient Greeks
they so adored their mythic beasts:
dragons, griffins, unicorns
manticores and minotaurs.

Egyptians though were not like that:
not only were they fond of cats
those funky sideways-stepping people
so revered the dung beetle.

Yes, those weeny minibeasts
on faeces they will only feast.
Why? – because it's full of fibre
free and there is nothing finer?

But why did the Egyptians love
those tiny backwards-rolling bugs?
They thought the beetle's daily run
was like the journey of the sun

Trundling through the sky all day
up so early, down so late
for them, the sun, a holy god
as were those busy beetle bods.

They called them *scarabs* – wore them too
to bring them luck – now wouldn't you?
They're super-powered – and absurd . . .
the strongest creature in the world!

Dragons? Griffins? Fiction stuff!
These eco-beetles, they're so tough
and rid the world of nastiness
they're really real and just the biz.
With holy rollers – who needs myths?

James

Glow Worms

Colour bombed the sky; orange, gold and crazy pink,
A sunset like the planet's very last
With clouds that melted into purple ink
So insanely luminous it made me gasp.
I drank it up until the last light left
And dropped me down into the mud and dark,
Where I shuffled, stone stumbling, bereft
Sunk back in sadness. Suddenly a spark
Showed at my feet, a tiny moon of neon green,
First one, then fifty and then all around.
Every other stalk had its own private gleam,
It looked as if the Milky Way had fallen to the ground,
And I was lifted up again by light
Born of Earth not sky, but still as bright.

Nicola

Woodlice

Underneath is where you'll find them
Anywhere it's damp and icky.
Coffin cutters, gammer sows
Always running from the sunlight
On their seven pairs of legs
Tiggy hogs and fairie's pigs.
Eating poo and rotting leaves.
Bibble bugs and pills and cudworms
Moist and dark is what they like,
They're the relatives of crabs and lobsters,
Perhaps they're looking for the sea?

Nicola

Dragon Fly

Forget princes, crowns and swordfights,
Your trade is water fleas,
Hog-lice, sticklebacks,
Terrorising tadpoles
In the pond's murk.
Your killing's done stone cold,
A grab and smash of bodies
That contribute to your bulk,
So you can shed your tight skin,
Only to outgrow another.

Will this apprenticeship be over?
Is it true you'll split this uniform
And finally ignite in sunshine?
Or is that just a fairy tale!

Nicola

Spider, Spider . . .

!
!
!
!
!
!
!

. . . hear my rhyme!
Do you think you'll spare

Spider, spider   the time to spin a little web to-   *Spider, spider*

night? From sticky silk in cold moon-

Spider, spider   light? You weave away. You scuttle free.   *Spider, spider*

Your artistry's an alchemy, of science, maths

and harmony. A masterpiece of symmetry. A

Spider, spider   clever, clinging web design. A classic, Gothic   *Spider, spider*

house divine. Your magic number? No surp-

rise. You have eight legs. You have eight

Spider, spider   eyes. Little dancer, have you heard?   *Spider, spider*

Your web's 8th Wonder

of the World . . .

!   !

James

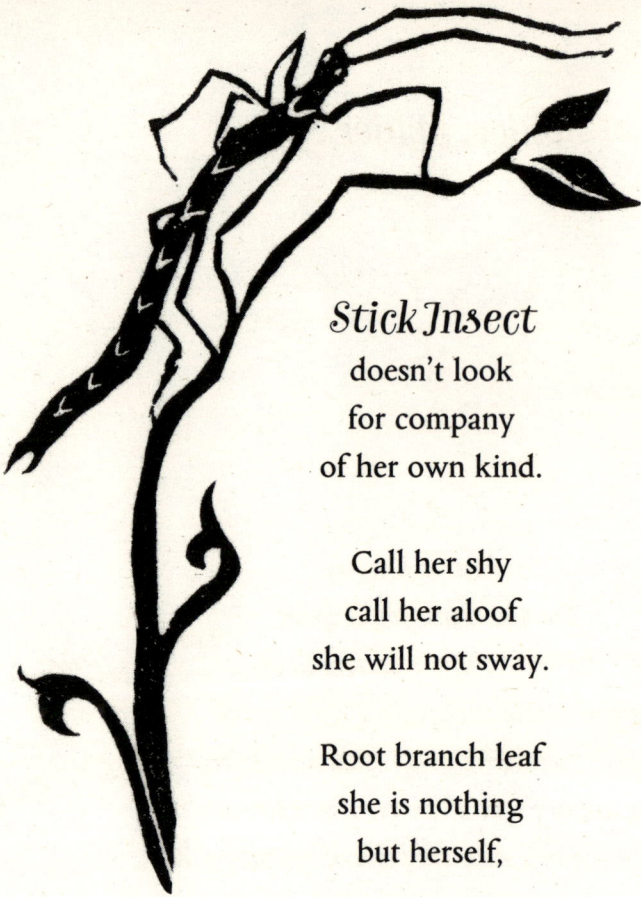

Stick Insect

doesn't look
for company
of her own kind.

Call her shy
call her aloof
she will not sway.

Root branch leaf
she is nothing
but herself,

turns up on plants
without an invite,
holds her nerve

against the wind.

Dom

Wonder

Whether you call it magic,
  a miracle or simply the workings
of science, all life is a sublime concoction;

an alchemy of brilliant contradictions.
  For born of the fire of our neighbouring
sun, all life is nothing but stardust. And yet

we mainly comprise of water, exist as
  conscious wetness; so – simultaneously
water and dust and fire? *That's life!*

                                        James

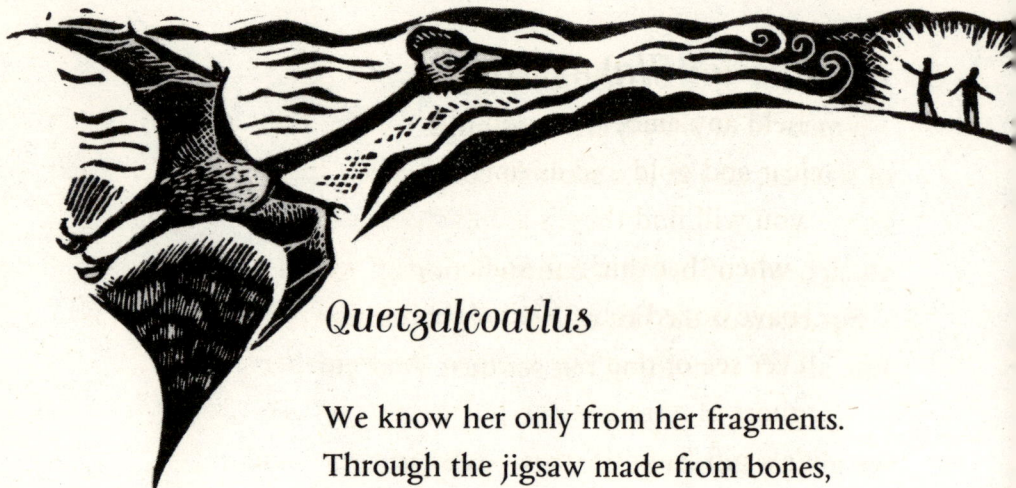

Quetzalcoatlus

We know her only from her fragments.
Through the jigsaw made from bones,
We see her standing at a river's edge,
Vast wings folded like a giant, broken brolly,
snatching trilobites with javelin jaws.
Or spiralling on leather wings,
spread wider than a house is high
her fingers hollow as a straw
to keep her light.

She lived before the mountains grew
before the meteor that changed the world
and gave our line its racing start.
She was dead for for sixty million years
Until one long finger poked into the light.
And now at the corner of an eye
At the edge of our imagination
Quetzalcoatlus casts a purple shadow
On the Texan dust.

Nicola

Have you ever

held any amber? A solid block of honey,
clear and gold, old as time? If you're lucky,
you will find there's a bug stuck inside –
when that thick 'n' sticky syrup would
have oozed then dried. And it's all we'll
ever see of that sky-scraper, forest-maker
ghost of a tree. Like a poem, built to last,
it's a gift from the past – now in your hand
a small reminder, yellow wonder,
precious chunk of ancient amber.

James

Up Uffington Hill

Each and every Spring they come,
   to climb the hill, to clean the chalk,

to leave the horse as white
   as they can for yet another year.

Locals, ramblers, families all, toil away
   with tools, with trowels, and all weekend

they'll work this mound, this chalkhill
   formed of countless shells that fell

to what was once an ocean floor.
   Though no one seems to know for sure

who created the horse or why. Now look
  at those legs. Outstretched. As if in flight.

So is it a supernatural horse? A spirit, free
  from gravity's reins, mortality's bones,

released to rise above these hills, far
  above the sleeping earth, beneath

the deepest ocean of them all, of stars?

James

Selkie Summoning

Come to me, my skin, my sliver
From the shade beneath the stone.
The land to me grows weary, dreary;
I would be gone.
Come to me, my skin, my other!
Find me lost upon the shore.
A storm of dark is in me;
I fight no more.
Come to me, my skin, my wildness!
I have wasted here too long.
Take my words and take my language,
Give me song.

Come to me, my skin of starlight,
So I may swim under the deep,
In the salt-blue of forgetting
I will sleep.

Nicola

Talking Hands

I've been thinking about those hands
    again. The ones on the walls in the caves
underground. And I'm wondering whether

they're warning – or waving – or simply
    just saying, *Hey, we were here too!*
It's easy for us. Thumbing our thoughts

onto our phones and instantly pinging them
    out to the world. They only had paint,
and those cold, stone walls. Imagine

touching one of those hands. Just
    for an instant. Greeting an ancestor
lost in time with a simple high-five.

For World Poetry Day, 21 March 2021.

James

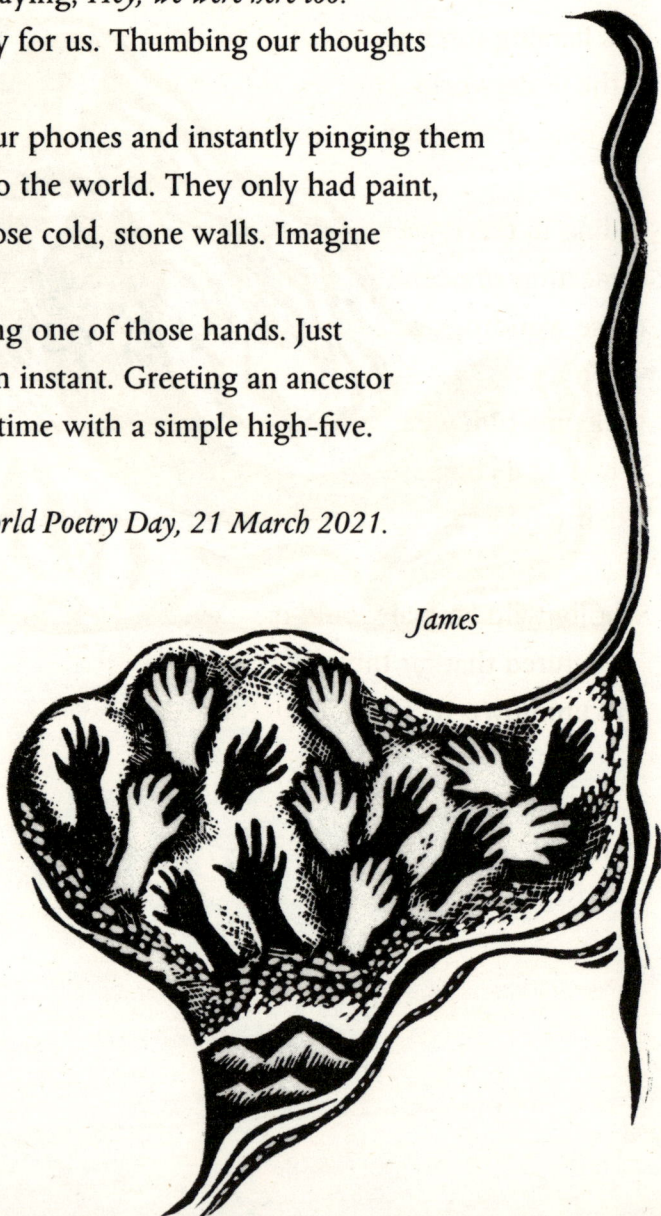

168

We'll never know
    for sure what the first ever pet was.
And yet it's clear that a boy went roaming —

far into a cave in Southern France,
    sometime in the final Ice Age. His
footprints remain, set in the stone floor.

His flaming torch guided him far into
    the underworld. He even slipped in
the mud at one point. Whether he was

hiding in there, seeking something,
    meeting someone, or on his way to view
those wondrous wall paintings already

millennia old, we'll never know. Though
    he had a companion for certain. A wolf.
Their tracks run side by side. Yet no

wholly wild animal would have ever
    ventured that far through the dark
and unknown with a human. So what

I want to know is this: had that trusting
   creature, one happy to wander deep
into the cold, shadowed earth – one

still wolf and not yet dog – been
   given a name by the boy?
If so, what was it?

                         James

Index of First Lines

3 a.m. and a hush of bin bags splits the night	15
A gannet's eyes are bluest blue	54
A honey-warm day and she carries me	148
A seed	90
A should always be for aardvark	104
A *stampede* of millipedes?	147
A tree is not like you or me	94
After we visited the zoo	24
Ancient tree of the sea	80
At home they would be flying South	57
AUTUMN's a breeze	91
Be still!	115
Can there be a Spring	109
Circle as you sleep, my love	46
Colour bombed the sky; orange, gold and crazy pink	152
Come On Out	128
Come to me, my skin, my sliver	166
Could you put your arms around a friend	34
Come, Crow – bring down the night	48
Dire warnings, melting icecaps	110
Do you remember	73
Each and every Spring they come	164
Even in the rain she'll be there	29
Every night she would dream	42
Forget princes, crowns and swordfights	154
Fox, what have you done?	119
Grass, GRASS	96

Have you ever   163

He sits and he stares   133

He taught me all the names for finch: 44

He was a solitary child   13

He's a high-pitched singer   82

Here comes   51

Home is wherever your spirit is free   142

Huge and sacred, my 'Book of Kells'   41

I love this parka in its big glass case   16

I wanted to be water   69

I'm asking who does the owl turn to   52

I've been thinking about those hands   168

I've known you since nursery   20

If I could give you just one place   68

If you've ever seen a wolf   124

In the tangerine sky above the station   43

Isn't it incredible   49

It turns out you won   140

It was not easy   35

It's like walking through a town at 2 a.m.   77

Kiaow! Kiaow!   55

Limpet, is it simple   74

Maukin, maigheach-gheal, mountain hare   116

Monkey doesn't seem to notice   136

Moon-bright, heart-light   56

Now it seems like a dream   70

Off Cabo Norte   53

On a walk   60

Once I've WOLFed   122

Once, on the blue side of the world   8

Our message is not written   17

Rain will fall and wind will blow   89

Rarely a day passes   72

Remember the day when we killed the bees   106

Rock is a sentence   37

Sailors squinting at their sonar screens   75

She watches the world   126

So full of yellow sunshine   97

Somewhere out there is that hare   117

Spider, Spider . . .   155

Stick Insect   156

Strength/Sun   27

Thanks to gravity, nothing ever   32

The deep, deep blue between the floes   79

The dogs lay behind the pig pen door, as still as stones 36

The first time she saw   141

The Romans and the Ancient Greeks   150

The sun pushes her cart past our window   31

The time my dog and I were stopped by a stranger   22

The Tree Whale crashed here long ago   92

The whale swims underneath the city   28

The white butterfly   149

The Winter storms have washed up a wonder   67

There will always still be sky   101

There's a path you must find   11

There's a rhythm out there   2

They look up at you with big eyes   102

They wouldn't leT you near it now   95

Though we are warmest in the womb   26
Two twigged feet pitch a fat green tent   62
Underneath is where you'll find them   153
We both had our minds on other things: 130
We know her only from her fragments   162
We live for the light   10
We'll never know   169
We've used this planet like a jakes   108
What colour are the hills?   9
When London's under twenty feet of sea   107
When Sun was young   118
when Whale dipped out of sight   84
Whenever you walk   98
Where on earth   138
Where sunlight sifts cliff and sky   45
Whether you call it magic   161
Which creature would you be?   85
Who are these nightlings   33
Who cares   105
who'd have thought a flame could find a home in water   14
Winter's creeping back   78
Without a name a goose   58
Yes, it was the Romans who   135
You're a rag, a bag   120
You're out there, in the wild,   7
Your voice low, you ask   23

About the Poets

James Carter is an award-winning children's poet, non-fiction writer and musician. An ambassador for National Poetry Day, he travels all over the UK and abroad with his melodica (that's *Steve*) and ukulele (that's *Erik*) to give lively performances and run creative poetry workshops – and above all, to get children and teachers excited about words.

Dom Conlon is a poet and author whose first two books were nominated for the Carnegie Medal. Through commissions for the BBC to being a UNESCO World Poetry Day poet, Dom continues to explore the many ways in which humans interact with and respond to the world around them.

Nicola Davies is a writer, producer and presenter of radio and television, including *The Really Wild Show*. Amongst her many acclaimed books for children are *Big Blue Whale*, *One Tiny Turtle*, and *Poo,* which was shortlisted for a Blue Peter Book Award.

About the Illustrator

Diana Catchpole is an illustrator and printmaker. She studied book illustration at the Cambridge School of Art and after graduating went on to illustrate children's books. She discovered printmaking in 2015 and the relief technique of linocut became her passion. She lives in Cambridgeshire and takes much of her inspiration from the surrounding countryside and the wild animals that inhabit it.

Acknowledgements

'Tree', 'The Light', 'Who cares', 'She Watches the World', 'Gorilla Gazing', and 'Elephant' from *Weird Wild & Wonderful* by James Carter copyright ©2021 published by Otter-Barry Books; 'The Monkey & The Apple', 'The Light', 'Crow', 'Seasons 4' and 'The Old Wood' from *The World's Greatest Space Cadet* by James Carter copyright ©2017 published by Bloomsbury; 'Somewhere' by James Carter was first published in *Poems For 8 Year Olds* by Matt Goodfellow (Macmillan); 'Talking Hands' by James Carter was first published in *Wonder: The Natural History Museum Poetry Book* by Ana Sampson (Macmillan); 'The Rhythm' is adapted from two stanzas of *Once Upon A Rhythm* by James Carter copyright ©2019 published by Little Tiger Press.